Woh Ek Saal

Prashant Bhardwaj

Published by Prashant Bhardwaj, 2025.

This is a work of fiction. Similarities to real people, places, or events are entirely coincidental.

WOH EK SAAL

First edition. November 29, 2025.

ISBN: 979-8230357759

Written by Prashant Bhardwaj.

Table of Contents

Woh Ek
Saal
A Journey of Love, Pain,
and Redemption
One year that changed everything
PRASHANT BHARDWAJ

Woh Ek Saal

A story of love, betrayal, and rediscovery

(One year that changed everything.)

"A Novel by Prashant Bhardwaj"

Chapter 1 – The First Meeting

The winter sun slipped through a veil of thin clouds, painting the school grounds with a soft, golden glow. Arav, twenty-two, adjusted the strap of his worn leather bag and stepped into the staff room. The familiar scent of chalk dust, the shuffle of papers, and the gentle clinking of teacups greeted him like an old routine.

Being the only male teacher in an all-female staff was never simple. It came with curious glances, light-hearted gossip, and occasionally, the protective stares of senior colleagues. Yet over time, Arav's quiet dignity and respectful manner had earned him an unspoken acceptance in these walls.

That morning, as he placed the attendance registers neatly on the table, the door creaked open. He looked up— and froze.

She walked in. Siya.

Her presence was like a sudden breeze drifting into a still room. Dressed in a light blue suit embroidered delicately at the sleeves, her hair tied in a neat braid that fell gracefully over her shoulder, she carried with her a sense of calmness, a rhythm untouched by the usual morning rush.

"Good morning," she said, her voice warm, though gently restrained.

Arav offered a faint smile. "Good morning. You must be the new English teacher?"

She returned the smile, placing her bag on the desk opposite his. "Yes. Siya Verma."

For a brief moment, her eyes lingered on his— not searching, not probing, simply observing. Then, with a quiet composure, she began arranging her notebooks. Arav noticed the way her fingers moved carefully, almost tenderly, as though every pen, every sheet of paper carried a story of its own.

The distant school bell rang, slicing through the stillness. Both of them stood, ready to step into their duties. Yet, as Arav walked out, he found himself glancing back at her.

Something about that first look— calm, fleeting, yet unshakable— had stirred a quiet curiosity in him. One that, in time, would grow into something far deeper than he could have ever imagined.

Chapter 2 – First Impressions

The next morning, the staffroom carried its usual hum—pages turning, chalk dust in the air, teachers murmuring over lesson plans. Arav sat at his desk, adjusting the register, when the principal walked in with a new face beside him.

"This is Siya Sharma," the principal announced warmly. "She will be joining us as a teacher from today."

All eyes turned toward her. Siya stood gracefully in a simple peach-colored suit, dupatta neatly draped. There was a quiet poise about her, a softness that made the room pause for a second. She offered a polite smile, folded her hands in greeting, and sat at the desk assigned to her.

Arav glanced up, curious. Something about her calm presence made her stand apart. For a moment, he forgot the clutter of registers before him. Their eyes met briefly, and he gave a small nod. Siya returned it, shy but assured.

During the break, as colleagues exchanged casual words with her, Arav found himself listening more than speaking. Siya's voice was clear, thoughtful, with an undercurrent of confidence.

Later in the day, Arav had to distribute new timetables. When he reached Siya's desk, she looked up with an earnest smile.

"Thank you, sir," she said politely, taking the sheet from him.

Arav noticed the respect in her tone. Sir. It carried sincerity, not formality.

"You've been allotted Class 6 and 7," he explained. "If you need any help with the students or the syllabus, feel free to ask."

"I will," Siya replied, her voice soft but steady. "This is my first appointment... I want to give my best."

For reasons he couldn't name, her words struck something inside him. He remembered his own first day at this school—how nervous yet determined he had been. Watching Siya reminded him of that beginning, of raw honesty before routine took over.

Over the next few days, their paths crossed naturally—passing in corridors, exchanging notes about schedules, small nods in the staffroom. Nothing more than professional courtesy, yet there was a gentle rhythm in these interactions.

One evening, as the final bell rang and the staffroom emptied, Arav noticed Siya struggling with a pile of books. Without a second thought, he stepped forward.

"Let me help," he said.

For a moment she hesitated, then allowed him to take half the stack. Their fingers brushed lightly against the covers, an ordinary touch, but it lingered in Arav's thoughts longer than he expected.

Walking side by side through the quiet corridor, neither spoke much. Yet, in the silence, an unspoken acknowledgment passed between them—something new had entered both their lives.

Arav didn't name it. Siya didn't either. But a seed had been planted, quietly, beneath the everyday routine of the school.

Chapter 3 – Circles of Trust

The Director's cabin was a modest space, lined with framed certificates and old photographs of students holding trophies with shining eyes. The air carried the faint aroma of cardamom tea, curling gently from the cup in the Director's hand. Seated comfortably in his chair, the man — in his early fifties, with kind eyes and a fatherly presence — looked up as the door opened.

Arav walked in without knocking, his step easy, familiar.

"Aaja, Arav," the Director said warmly, setting his cup down. "You don't need to knock. You're like family here."

Arav grinned. "Sir, one should always knock before entering your cabin."

They laughed softly — the kind of laughter that belonged to bonds older than the moment. The Director reached for another cup, poured tea with practiced hands, and slid it across the desk. Arav accepted it with quiet gratitude.

"You're not just a teacher working for me," the Director said, his voice steady yet affectionate. "You're like a younger brother. My doors — even my home — are always open for you. I trust you completely."

The words carried weight. They weren't flattery; they were truth shaped by years.

Arav lowered his gaze for a moment before meeting the older man's eyes. "Sir, you've given me the love of a younger brother and trusted me. I've learned so much from you... especially how to stand firm when times are tough."

"That's why I handed my beloved school to you," the Director replied, pride softening his tone. "Whatever decision you make, I believe it will be the right one."

They sat together in silence, sipping tea. It was not an empty silence but one that spoke of bonds unshaken by time.

Arav placed his cup down gently. "The trust you have in me — I will never let it break."

The Director's eyes gleamed with quiet pride. No more words were needed.

—-

Across the building, the staffroom buzzed with lighter voices and the clink of spoons against porcelain cups. Sunlight slanted through half-drawn curtains, painting warm rectangles on the floor where three young teachers sat huddled together.

Sandhya leaned forward, lowering her voice. "Did you notice? Arav sir just walked into the Director's cabin without knocking."

Gautami chuckled. "That place is like his second home. If the Director is having tea, he'll pour one for Arav too. They sit together all day. He's the Director's most trusted person now."

Devika nodded. "Oh, it's more than that. The Director considers him a younger brother — that's why he has full access. No rules."

Sandhya smirked. "And have you seen his confidence? He walks around as if the school belongs to him."

"Not confidence," Gautami corrected, "influence. He makes the important decisions — admissions, hiring, even timetable changes."

"Everyone goes to him with their problems," Devika added. "Even the students adore him. The rest of us? We're just... teachers in name."

Sandhya sighed. "Still, no one dares misbehave in his class. Students sit quietly and actually listen. Whether that's out of respect or fear, I don't know."

"And us?" Gautami's voice dropped, tinged with resignation. "We're just chalk and boards."

Devika tilted her head, smiling faintly. "Sometimes it feels like we don't exist here. Only him. Though..." she paused, her smile turning sly, "he does look good too."

Sandhya rolled her eyes, though her voice softened. "One thing is certain — he works harder than all of us. Even on holidays, he comes to school. Who knows how much he loves this place."

"That's true," Gautami admitted. "But he's set a standard none of us can reach."

Devika's smile carried a hint of bitterness. "He's everyone's favorite — staff, students, even parents."

Sandhya raised a brow. "You like him too, yet here you are gossiping about him with me. That, madam, I don't quite understand."

The three fell silent, sipping their tea — caught somewhere between admiration, envy, and unspoken longing.

"I wish," Gautami murmured, almost to herself, "someone would say to me: 'The school doesn't feel right without you.'"

Devika leaned closer, her tone soft. "Don't worry. One day your time will come. Right now, it's Arav sir's time."

Their quiet laughter filled the staffroom, but beneath it lingered a tangle of rivalry and reluctant respect — the kind that often grows in the shadow of someone who shines too brightly.

Chapter 4 – Principal's Office

The morning sun streamed gently through the half-drawn curtains, painting golden slivers across the polished desk where Arav sat. The principal's office smelled faintly of paper and ink, with files neatly stacked, registers spread before him, and his pen gliding across a page in disciplined strokes.

The door opened with a soft creak. Siya stepped in, her presence quiet yet distinct. She wore a pale blue suit that matched the freshness of the morning, her braid resting neatly against her shoulder. In her hands she clutched a folder, the way one might hold something both fragile and important.

Arav looked up, his expression calm, touched with a polite warmth.

"Good morning. You're Siya, right?"

She nodded lightly. "Yes, sir. I'm here to submit my documents, as instructed."

"Great," he said, gesturing toward the chair opposite. "Please, have a seat."

"Thank you, sir."

Her voice carried a soft steadiness as she sat, placing the folder across the desk. Arav opened it, scanning the papers with the practiced eye of someone who valued order.

"Marksheet... internship certificate... identity proof... all in order." His brow lifted slightly as he turned the pages. "Your academic scores are consistent. That's good."

A modest smile touched Siya's lips. "I've always tried to be regular with my studies, sir. I believe discipline reflects in everything we do."

Arav glanced up. Something in her words seemed to linger, like a truth he silently agreed with.

"Spoken like a teacher already."

She dipped her head in acknowledgment.

He turned another page. "This is your teaching practicum report?"

"Yes, sir. I handled English and Moral Science during my final semester."

"Good," he replied, leaning back slightly. "You might be assisting with both here too. But classes will be assigned according to student needs. You comfortable with that?"

"Absolutely, sir. I'm here to learn and contribute however I can."

There was a pause—brief but weighty. Her sincerity was unforced, and it softened the formality of the conversation.

"This profession," Arav said, his tone reflective, "needs patience more than anything else. Talent helps, but patience... earns respect."

Siya's gaze warmed, her voice gentler now. "I understand. My mother is a teacher too. I've seen her give her life to this work."

His expression shifted almost imperceptibly—recognition passing between them like a quiet thread.

"Then you already know," he murmured, "that this isn't just a job. It's a responsibility."

Closing the folder, he set it neatly aside. "Alright. Your joining is processed. Report to the staff room after assembly. Ms. Devika will guide you."

"Yes, sir. Thank you for the opportunity."

"Welcome to the team, Siya."

Their eyes met briefly—professional, yet touched by something more. Neither named it. Neither lingered. But when Siya rose and walked to the door, Arav found himself watching her for a moment longer than necessary, before pulling his attention back to the open registers.

The room, somehow, felt quieter after she left.

Chapter 5 – The Staff Room

The new school's staff room was quieter than Siya expected—quieter, but not in a comforting way. The walls were bare, the furniture functional, the air carrying a formality that seemed to hush even laughter into something restrained. A long table stretched across the center, lined with chairs.

Siya sat near one end, her lunchbox still closed, her hands resting lightly on her lap. She wasn't part of the conversation—at least, not yet. She only listened as Sandhya, Gautami, and Devika exchanged words in the familiar rhythm of gossip.

"You haven't worked here with Arav sir before," Sandhya began with a scoff, "that's why you don't know much about him. Uff—he's extremely rude."

Gautami nodded eagerly. "Yes! Always piling on work. No peace. And all the pressure... it's always on us teachers."

"And Director sir," Devika added, her tone edged with sarcasm, "acts as if Arav sir is God. Doesn't listen to anyone else."

Sandhya rolled her eyes, recalling. "Once, I asked for a short leave. Arav sir gave me a lecture instead—'Don't compromise on your values.' As if I need to hear that every single day."

Gautami smirked. "And he never smiles. Just work, work, work. Sometimes I wonder if he even has a heart."

Devika gave a little laugh. "The students worship him though. All day it's, 'Arav sir said this,' 'Arav sir did that.' It's exhausting."

Sandhya leaned back in her chair, her tone half mocking, half bitter. "He walks around as if he's the best at everything... and we're just extras in his story."

Through it all, Siya's fingers played absently with the corner of her dupatta. Her face remained neutral, but her mind shifted—from listening, to weighing, to feeling the faint tug of discomfort.

Then Gautami turned, her gaze sharp with curiosity. "You've spent time with him. Tell me—are they right? Is he really that strict?"

Siya hesitated. Her words were careful, deliberate. "Yes... he is strict. But he's serious about his work. Maybe that's why... everyone respects him."

"Respect or fear?" Devika teased, arching a brow.

The question lingered.

Sandhya leaned in, eyes narrowing with playful intrigue. "But tell us this—when you worked with him before... how was the tuning between you two?"

For a second, Siya's composure faltered. Her eyes lowered, and her reply came softer than the rest.

"Professional thi. Bas."

The answer slipped into the silence, plain yet carrying an undertone no one could quite name. The three women exchanged glances, unsatisfied but unwilling to press further. Siya kept her gaze on her dupatta, memories brushing at the edges of her mind like shadows she wasn't ready to face.

"Alright, enough of old stories," Gautami said suddenly, forcing brightness into her tone. "So, who brought what for lunch today?"

The mood shifted. Laughter returned, punctuated with talk of parathas, pickles, and curries. The room warmed with everyday chatter.

But Siya remained quiet. Her lunchbox unopened, her thoughts drifting somewhere far away—back to a time she wasn't sure she wanted to revisit.

Chapter 6 – Echoes in the Rain

The afternoon corridors were quieter than usual, filled only with the shuffle of shoes and the low hum of students changing classes. Sunlight slanted through high windows, catching the dust motes that drifted lazily in the air.

Siya walked slowly, a small stack of notebooks balanced against her hip. Her mind was somewhere between the lesson she had just finished and the one she still needed to prepare.

As she turned a corner, she spotted three students — Bhoomi, Ishika, and Divyanshi — standing near the staircase. Their heads were bent together, voices alive with the warmth of shared memories.

"I really miss Arav sir's class," Bhoomi sighed. "He made everything so simple."

"Yes!" Ishika chimed in. "His examples were so funny—always something creative you'd never forget."

"Best teacher ever," Divyanshi added with a sincerity that stilled Siya's steps. "He never shouted, never underestimated anyone. It's just... no one can replace him."

Siya found herself slowing near the notice board, pretending to study the latest circulars though her ears stayed tuned.

"And his nature," Bhoomi continued, "was so calm. If we made a mistake, he would explain it—never scolded us."

Ishika's tone softened. "He wasn't just a teacher... he was a mentor."

"Wish he'd come back," Divyanshi murmured. "Now there's no excitement in waiting for any class."

The three girls drifted down the hallway, laughing at some memory only they understood.

Siya remained by the notice board, her gaze fixed but her thoughts elsewhere.
Maybe I judged him too quickly...
The thought was quiet, reluctant, but it lodged itself deeper than she expected.

—-

Later that day, the sky broke into a steady monsoon rain. The corridors echoed with the rush of water against tin roofs, the air cool and fragrant with wet earth.
Arav stood beneath the shelter of the covered walkway, watching the sheets of rain curtain the school grounds. For a rare moment, there was peace in the sound.
"Beautiful, isn't it?"
The voice was soft, familiar. Siya had appeared beside him, clutching a small steel tiffin. Her hair clung damply to her shoulders from the dash across the open yard.
Arav smiled faintly. "Yes. Rain always feels like a fresh start."
She studied him for a moment, then asked, "Do you believe in that? Fresh starts?"
He thought before answering. "Not always completely. But I believe we can choose how the next chapter goes."
Her lips curved into the faintest smile. "You talk like a writer, Arav sir."
"And you listen like one," he replied without thinking.
A soft laugh escaped her, carrying lightly into the sound of the rain. For a heartbeat, the air between them shifted—warm despite the chill.
But then another teacher passed by, giving them a curious glance. Siya noticed. The smile vanished, replaced by restraint. She held her tiffin closer. "I should get back," she said quickly, and walked away before he could respond.

—-

That evening, as Arav locked up the school office, Lovely appeared at the gate with an umbrella.

"She talks about you," Lovely said casually, eyes sharp.

He paused, the key still in his hand. "Siya?"

"Who else?" Lovely shrugged. "She's careful, doesn't want anyone to notice... but I can tell."

Arav gave no reply. He only adjusted his bag and stepped out into the rain.

Behind him, Lovely's voice drifted through the downpour, half a tease, half a warning.

"Careful, Arav. Not all rain is a blessing."

Chapter 7 – A Shared Task

The following morning, the school bustled with the usual Monday energy—students rushing through corridors, teachers hurrying with lesson plans, and the faint smell of chalk dust hanging in the air.

Arav sat at his desk in the staff room, updating attendance records, when the Principal entered, scanning the room.

“Arav sir, Siya madam—could you both help me prepare the activity boards for tomorrow’s cultural event? I need the displays ready by evening.”

Siya, who had just walked in with a neatly folded dupatta draped over her shoulder, nodded politely. Arav glanced at her and offered a quick smile, still recalling their rain-soaked conversation.

“Of course, sir,” Arav replied.

Together they carried stacks of colored charts, paints, and craft supplies to the empty auditorium. The afternoon sun streamed in through the high windows, casting golden streaks across the polished floor.

As they began cutting borders for the charts, Siya broke the silence.

“You’re surprisingly quick at this,” she said, watching him measure and trim with practiced ease.

“I’ve been doing this since my college fest days,” he said with a grin. “Back then, if you didn’t do it yourself, it never got done right.”

She laughed softly, shaking her head. “So you’re a perfectionist.”

“Not really,” Arav replied, pressing a strip of glitter paper neatly onto a chart. “I just like things to be... complete.”

There was a pause—comfortable, unhurried. The rhythmic snip of scissors and the faint hum of the ceiling fan filled the space.

At one point, their hands brushed while reaching for the same marker. Siya's fingers lingered just a fraction longer than necessary. Neither commented, but both felt the moment settle between them.

By evening, the boards stood finished—bright, detailed, and perfectly arranged.

"You know," Siya said as they stepped back to admire the work, "if the kids don't win the first prize tomorrow, it'll be the judges' fault."

Arav smiled. "I'll take that as a compliment."

They left the auditorium together, walking side by side. Outside, the cool breeze carried the faint scent of jasmine from the school garden. Neither spoke much, but there was a quiet sense of something beginning—like the first drops of rain before a monsoon.

Chapter 8 – The Colors Between Them

The festival of Holi arrived with a burst of laughter, colors, and sweet chaos. The school courtyard transformed into a canvas of joy—students chasing each other with gulal, teachers exchanging greetings, and the air filled with the fragrance of gujiyas and thandai.

Arav stood by, smiling as he watched the children play, his kurta already dusted with streaks of pink and green. Amid the noise, his eyes instinctively searched—and found Siya, radiant in a simple white salwar suit that now bore splashes of bright hues. She looked carefree, laughing with her friends, her bangles jingling as she threw colors in the air.

Their eyes met for a fleeting moment. For reasons neither could explain, the crowd and the laughter around them seemed to blur. Siya, cheeks flushed more from emotion than gulal, walked towards him, holding a pinch of pink powder in her hand.

"Happy Holi, sir," she said softly, hesitating only for a second before gently smearing the gulal across his cheek.

Arav smiled, warmth in his eyes. "Happy Holi, Siya," he replied, his voice steady and kind.

For a heartbeat, she waited—almost expecting him to return the gesture. But Arav, though tempted, only folded his hands in greeting with a gentle nod.

No... she is my student. Boundaries must remain, he reminded himself, even as a trace of longing flickered in his chest.

Siya lowered her eyes, masking the faint disappointment with a smile. She laughed lightly and turned back to her friends, but in her palm, a small pinch of untouched gulal remained—a gesture unfinished, a connection left unspoken.

Amid the riot of colors, a quiet shade settled between them. Neither bright nor dark—just something unnameable, lingering in the space they shared.

Chapter 9 – After the Colors Fade

The school courtyard looked almost bare now. Only faint streaks of pink and green clung stubbornly to the cement, ghostly reminders of yesterday's chaos. The laughter of Holi was gone, replaced by the rustle of papers and the faint squeak of chalk.

Arav walked through the corridor with his usual calm. His shirt sleeves still carried a faint purple stain near the cuff—he didn't notice it. Others did.

At the staffroom door, Siya sat arranging answer sheets, her hair tied neatly today, though a few strands had slipped loose near her temple—the same ones Arav had brushed colors into yesterday. She felt their eyes before she heard their voices.

Two teachers near the cupboard lowered their tone just enough to make it obvious.

"You saw them, right? In the courtyard?"

"Hmm... a little too friendly, I'd say."

Siya's pen froze mid-mark. She didn't turn, but her ears burned.

Arav entered then, offering a steady "Good morning" to everyone. His voice was even, unaffected. Siya didn't look up, but when he passed her desk, her hand shifted instinctively to hide the small smile tugging at her lips.

At lunch, Lovely plopped down beside her with a grin. "So... enjoyed Holi?"

Siya kept her tone neutral. "It was nice. Everyone had fun."

Lovely leaned in, teasing. "Everyone? Or just you and a certain someone?"

Siya's spoon paused above her plate. "Lovely..." she warned softly. But Lovely only chuckled, clearly pleased with herself.

By the time school ended, Siya was restless. She didn't like being the subject of whispers—yet the memory of Arav's quiet smile, his careful but warm presence under that neem tree, kept returning unbidden.

That night, while reviewing lesson plans on her bed, she noticed a faint smudge of pink on the corner of her notebook. She rubbed it away quickly... but couldn't stop smiling in the dark.

—-

Chapter 10 – Unspoken Confessions

Evening had settled quietly over the town, painting the sky in fading gold and deepening shades of blue. In his room, Arav lay stretched out on his bed, one hand tucked behind his head. Earphones rested in his ears, but no music played. His phone glowed softly in his other hand, the screen fixed on one thing—

the small green dot beside Siya's name.

She was online.

For a long moment, neither typed. Then, her message appeared.

SIYA: You post some pretty intense Insta stories!

A faint smile touched Arav's lips as his thumbs moved.

ARAV: If the question is heavy, the answer has to be just as strong.

The typing dots blinked. Paused. Then appeared again.

SIYA: By the way... can I ask you something?

ARAV: Of course. Always.

SIYA: How do I look to you?

Arav froze. His thumb hovered above the keypad. He read the question twice, weighing each possible reply, knowing his words could linger far longer than he intended. Finally, he began to type.

ARAV: Honestly... you're sweet, sorted, and graceful.

A beat.

SIYA: Just that much?

ARAV: What else can I say? If I start thinking about you, I could keep writing all night.

SIYA: Then write it down... what are you thinking?

Arav sat up now, no longer casual. The words came easier, flowing straight from the place he kept locked most tightly.

ARAV: Your eyes... they talk. And when you smile, it feels like everything is going to be okay.
SIYA: (blushing emoji) No one has ever said it like that before.
ARAV: Because you're different from everyone else.
SIYA: And you... you're the most honest of all.
ARAV: I love talking to you... it feels like the whole world comes to a standstill.
SIYA: Same here... I wait for your message every day.
ARAV: Really?
SIYA: Haan... aur jab late reply dete ho toh... thoda gussa bhi aata hai.
ARAV: Sorry, baccha. From now on, you're at the very top of my priority list.
SIYA: (heart emoji) Baccha?
ARAV: You're my life... and also my baby.
SIYA: And me?
ARAV: You're not just a like... I really, really like you. Maybe even more than that.
The dots blinked. Stopped. Blinked again.
SIYA: Can I ask for something?
ARAV: You have every right over me.
SIYA: I want to talk to you every day... without any reason.
ARAV: That's an order... I'm ready. Every day. All the time.
SIYA: Really?
ARAV: Truly. My happiness lies in your happiness.
There was a long pause. Then, slowly—
SIYA: People like you are rare... or maybe there's only one.
Arav read her words again and again, his chest tightening with something he couldn't name, but felt more certain of with every heartbeat.

Chapter 11 – The Protector

Siya sat cross-legged on her bed, wrapped in a soft night suit, the pale yellow lamplight pooling around her. Her hair hung loosely over her shoulders, but her face looked drained — eyes heavy, smile forced.

The phone screen flickered to life. Arav's face appeared, grinning at first.

"Hey, babe! What's with that face? You look... tense. Everything okay?"

"I'm fine," she said, trying to sound casual. "Just tired, that's all."

His smile faded into a frown. "No, you're not fine. I can see it. Don't lie to me, Siya. Did something happen? Tell me, please."

Her gaze faltered. "It's nothing, really... please don't worry."

"Come on, Siya," he said gently, voice softer now. "I know you better than that. You're not just tired. Did someone say something? Did something happen at school?"

Her lips trembled. She looked away from the camera, blinking hard.

"Siya..." Arav's voice dropped to a murmur. "I won't force you. If you don't want to tell me, it's okay. But just know I'm here for you."

She sniffled, shaking her head. "No, no... I'm not crying because of you. It's just... yesterday, while I was walking home from school, two boys on a bike started following me."

His expression shifted instantly — concern sharpening into something darker. "What? What did they do?"

"They were commenting on me... saying things. I ignored them, but it felt so disgusting. I was scared." Her voice cracked. "I didn't tell you yesterday because I knew you'd get angry."

"Angry?" Arav's tone flared, his jaw tightening. "I'm beyond angry, Siya. Who were those bastards? I swear I'll break their faces. You should have told me yesterday itself!"

She dabbed at her tears while he clenched his fists, his fury barely contained.
"Tomorrow," he said firmly, his voice brooking no argument, "you're not going alone. I'll be there. I'll find those jerks."

—

The next evening, the school gate clanged open and Siya stepped out, clutching her bag close. Her eyes darted up and down the road, scanning every shadow. The ordinary walk home now felt like a battlefield.
A few steps behind, dressed in a plain T-shirt, cap pulled low, and sunglasses masking his face, Arav followed quietly, blending into the background like a silent guard.
The low rumble of a bike engine broke the quiet. Siya froze as two familiar figures rolled into view, cutting across her path.
"Look who's here again... Miss Pretty Teacher," the one in front sneered.
"Why don't you smile for us, baby?" the other added, his grin twisted.
Siya instinctively stepped back, her heart thudding — but before they could inch closer, a voice thundered through the air.
"HEY!"
Arav stormed forward like a force of nature. In one swift motion, he grabbed the pillion rider by the collar and yanked him clean off the bike. The rider tried to speed away, but Arav's boot smashed against the side of the bike, sending it toppling with a crash. Both boys sprawled to the ground.
"You think it's funny to harass girls?!" Arav's voice roared, raw with rage. "You messed with the wrong person!"
His fist connected hard with one boy's jaw, sending him reeling. The other lunged at him, but Arav sidestepped with precision, driving his knee into the boy's stomach until he doubled over in pain.
A crowd was beginning to gather now — murmurs rising, phones lifting, recording.

"Arav! Stop!" Siya's voice cut through the chaos, laced with panic. "Someone might call the police!"

Arav grabbed one boy by the collar, pulling him close enough to hear every word. His eyes blazed. "If I ever see you near her again, you'll regret being born."

He shoved them back, his strength radiating in every movement. The boys scrambled, stumbling over each other in their desperate rush to escape.

The world seemed to pause. Breathing heavily, Arav turned to Siya. His voice softened, the storm within him giving way to something gentler. "You're safe now. I won't let anyone hurt you again."

Her throat tightened, gratitude flooding her eyes. Without thinking, she stepped forward and wrapped her arms around him. His embrace was firm, steady, unyielding — the kind of hold that told her she was no longer alone, no longer unprotected.

For Siya, the world had been cruel just moments ago. But in his arms, it felt whole again.

Chapter 12 – First Outing and Shattered Calm

"Siya... The weekend morning sun cast a cheerful glow over the city as Arav and Siya stepped into the bustling shopping mall. The hum of weekend shoppers, soft background music, and the vibrant atmosphere of summer filled the air. Though both were slightly awkward, their excitement was undeniable—it was their first outing together, and both wanted to make it unforgettable.

Arav wore a light blue shirt with jeans, simple yet neat. Siya walked beside him in a traditional blue suit, her silver earrings swaying as she adjusted her slipping dupatta. They shared shy smiles, every glance carrying the promise of a new beginning.

Stopping in front of a clothing store, Siya picked up two kurtis—one pastel pink with delicate floral embroidery, the other navy blue adorned with mirror work.

"Is this kurti nice, or the other one?" she asked, holding both out for his opinion.

Arav tilted his head, pretending to be a fashion expert. "Hmm... this pink one looks more beautiful. Just like you—soft and classy."

Siya raised an amused eyebrow. "Classy? You seem to be quite the expert when it comes to clothes!"

"Oh, I'm just guessing based on your expressions," Arav replied, smiling. "By the way, the blue one would suit you too—it gives a strong, bold look."

"So you're saying I'm soft sometimes, and bold at other times?" she teased.

"Exactly. Depends on the mood. But both versions are nice," he said warmly.

Touched by his attention, Siya held the pink kurti closer and nodded. "Alright, I'll take this one. Your first outing suggestion turned out to be a good one."

—-

Later, in the food court, they sat at a small table laden with chaat, cold drinks, and ice cream. Siya laughed as Arav struggled with a particularly spicy golgappa.

"This one burned all the way from the tongue to the heart!" he coughed, eyes watering.

"Arre, that was the mild version! You definitely need training," she teased, giggling.

"Well, you're perfect for the training—the spicy teacher herself!" he shot back.

Siya smirked. "You're like butter chicken. I'm all spicy and tangy. How will we ever match?"

"Opposites attract, na?" he said softly. Their eyes met, and a warm smile spread across both faces—a moment light and yet deeply real.

—-

A short walk later brought them to a park, where children ran freely and a balloon vendor called out in the distance. Sitting under a gulmohar tree with petals scattered around, Siya whispered, "For the first time, I feel so comfortable with someone... without any pressure."

"Me too," Arav replied. "Time just stops when I'm with you. I forget about work, about stress—everything."

Glancing at him, Siya felt a blush rise to her cheeks. "You really are different, Arav. Guys these days only talk... but you... you truly understand."

"I just speak from the heart. And with you, it feels even easier," he murmured.

A sudden gust of wind blew Siya's dupatta, and Arav quickly held it for her, handing it back gently. "It seems even the weather wants you to trust me a little more."

Siya smiled faintly. "With time... anything is possible." Their eyes locked, and in that quiet pause, something undeniable began to take shape.

—-

Evening fell, and rain poured relentlessly over the city streets. Arav rode his bike through the empty, wet roads, focused and careful, the chill of the rain stinging his face. His phone vibrated in his pocket, but he didn't check it.

Meanwhile, in her room, Siya sat cross-legged on her bed, the glow of her lamp casting shadows across her anxious face. Her fingers trembled as she typed:

> "Where are you? Why aren't you seeing my texts?"

No reply. Her heart tightened. She dialed his number.

"Hello?" Arav's voice came, calm yet strained. "I'll call you later... I'm riding."

"You're riding the bike and picked the call?! Are you out of your mind?!" Siya exclaimed, half-angry, half-fearful.

"I didn't want to ignore you," he replied softly.

Her voice wavered. "Idiot... if anything happens to you, what will I do? Please, keep the phone away. Ride slowly. I love you... meri jaan."

A smile broke across his face. "I love you too... baccha."

And then—a sudden, loud screech. A thunderous crash.

"Arav?! What was that sound?!" Siya screamed, her chest tightening. No reply. "Please... say something... Arav!"

An unfamiliar female voice answered. "Hello? Are you... someone close to him?"

"Yes! Yes, I'm Siya! Please tell me what happened! Is he okay?!"

"He met with an accident. I was passing by and saw him unconscious, lying in the rain," the voice said.

Siya's world spun. "No... no, no! Is he breathing?! Is he bleeding?! Please tell me!"

"He had minor injuries. I sprinkled water on his face... he opened his eyes. He wants to talk to you."

A faint voice came through the speaker. "Siya... don't cry... I'm okay."

"Aarav?! Oh God! Are you in pain? I'm coming! Tell me where you are!"

"No... you don't need to come. Just wait for me, please. I'll be fine. I'll talk to you again... okay?"

"Please... don't cut the call... I need to hear your voice!"

CLICK. The call disconnected.

Siya collapsed onto her bed, sobs breaking through her trembling hands. "Arav... please come back... please..."

—

Two hours later, rain still hammering the windows, her phone buzzed.

> "I'm home now. So no need to panic. Relax, okay?"

Her hands shook as she typed furiously:

> You messaged me after two hours?! Don't you have any sense?! I was terrified to lose you!

The reply came instantly:

> Hey, don't cry. I'm fine.

She pressed the video call button. Arav appeared on the screen—pale, with a bandage on his forehead, but alive. Tears streamed down Siya's cheeks.

"How did this happen?! Why didn't you listen to me?!" she cried. "I told you so many times—if you're riding, don't use your phone!"

"I'm sorry... I didn't mean to hurt you," he whispered.

Through tears, she said, "I don't care about the mistake... I care about you."

"I love you, baccha," he murmured.
"I love you more... idiot," she whispered back.

—-

Ten days later, sunlight streamed through Arav's room. The bandage on his forehead was smaller now. On his table lay a tiffin, a folded handkerchief, and a note:
> "Take it easy. Don't rush anything. — Siya ?"
He smiled faintly, feeling the warmth of a love that had survived the storm.

—-

Montage: Six Months of Happiness
Sharing lunches in the staff room, Siya sneaking him bites from her tiffin.
Late-night phone calls filled with laughter and sleepy whispers.
Notes tucked into notebooks, secret meetings under the terrace sky.
Quiet promises whispered in the breeze:
"You'll stay with me always, right?"
"As long as I breathe," Arav replied.

For a while, life was nothing but soft days and unshaken dreams.
But fate was waiting.
One ordinary morning, Arav entered the staff room, humming—only to find Siya's desk empty.
"Siya ma'am didn't come?" he asked a colleague.
Gautami shook her head. "Arey Arav, you don't know? Siya resigned yesterday."
The ground shifted under him. "Resigned?"
Later, outside the school gate, he saw her. Siya walked quickly, eyes avoiding his.
"You didn't even tell me?" he asked, voice breaking.

"I... I was troubled by the staff's taunts," she whispered. "Every day... they said I get special treatment because of you..."

"So you thought hiding our love was the answer?" His voice cracked with hurt. "You know how deeply I feel for you."

Her eyes glistened with guilt, but she remained silent and kept walking.

don't go... please stop..." Arav's words dissolved into the evening air.

The first outing, the accident, the tender months—they all seemed like a fragile dream now, shattering in the face of cruel reality.

Chapter 13 – A New Beginning

The morning sun cast a gentle glow over the gates of Shanti Memorial School. The wide iron gates stood tall, freshly painted, and behind them, the campus buzzed with life. Groups of students in crisp uniforms hurried past, their laughter ringing through the air. The faint melody of the assembly prayer still lingered like an echo, blending with the rustle of leaves overhead.

Siya paused for a moment at the gate, adjusting the strap of her pastel pink suit. The soft fabric swayed with the breeze, her new handbag brushing lightly against her side. In her other hand, she clutched a neatly packed lunchbox her mother had insisted she carry. She took a deep breath, her eyes lifting toward the three-storied school building. Though her face radiated quiet determination, her fingers betrayed her nerves, tightening around the strap of her bag as though it were her anchor.

First day. New beginnings. Just breathe, she reminded herself.

Inside, the staffroom was alive with its own rhythm. Wooden chairs scraped against the floor as teachers moved around. The shuffle of papers mixed with the occasional sound of chalk snapping against the blackboard in nearby classrooms. Somewhere in the corner, a kettle whistled softly, releasing the rich smell of fresh tea that filled the air. Siya stepped inside cautiously, her eyes sweeping across unfamiliar faces.

A cheerful woman in her thirties, round-faced with bright eyes, looked up and smiled warmly.

"Welcome, Siya! First day?"

"Yes, first day," Siya replied, her voice gentle yet slightly uncertain. "Hoping to survive it."

Before the woman could respond, another figure leaned in. She was tall, with a sparkle in her eyes and a mischievous smile that made her presence instantly felt.

"Don't worry, you'll love it here. I'm Lovely, and I sit just over there," she said, pointing to a desk near the wide window, where sunlight poured in. "Come, I'll show you around."

There was something about Lovely's tone—effortless, warm, and slightly playful—that immediately put Siya at ease. The tension in her shoulders eased, her steps becoming lighter as she followed her new colleague through the room.

Within minutes, the two were chatting like they'd known each other for years instead of minutes. Lovely cracked lighthearted jokes about the principal's obsession with perfectly aligned noticeboards and how he inspected them as though they were military drills. Siya couldn't help but laugh, an honest, unguarded laugh that surprised even herself. It was a sound she hadn't allowed to escape her lips in weeks, not since life had begun to weigh heavily on her heart.

For the first time, she didn't feel like a stranger. She felt... at home

—

Chapter 13A – Shifting Currents

That night, Arav lay sprawled on his bed, one arm tucked under his head, the ceiling fan spinning lazily above him. His phone rested against his ear, Siya's voice trickling into the quiet of his room like music he never wanted to stop. There was something different about her tone tonight—lighter, freer, almost playful.

"Arav, you know what?" she said, giggling softly. "I don't even go to the canteen without Lovely. She's literally like my school soul sister now!"

Arav chuckled, the sound warm and teasing. "Acha? So has Lovely become more important than me now?"

"Drama queen," Siya teased, rolling her eyes though he couldn't see it. "You two are in completely different categories. But you... you're the closest to my heart."

Her words were simple, but they carried a weight that sank deep into Arav's chest. His smile deepened, a quiet reassurance washing over him. He believed her—without hesitation, without doubt.

—-

Later that week, the staffroom at Shanti Memorial was buzzing between classes. Teachers shuffled through notes, sipped tea, and exchanged quick conversations about students. Siya sat at her desk, her dupatta draped neatly across her shoulder, her posture calm yet graceful.

Beside her sat a tall, easygoing man in his late twenties. His name was Krunal, and he had a way of carrying himself that drew people in without him even trying. His sleeves were rolled up, revealing lean forearms, and his smile seemed to linger longer than necessary.

"So, Madam Siya," he began with a grin, tilting his head slightly, "do the kids get bored during your history class... or do you bore them?"

She laughed, her hand brushing a strand of hair from her face. "I teach with all my heart. If they're getting bored, that's their problem."

Krunal's eyes glimmered with amusement as he leaned back casually in his chair. "By the way... your smile is very distracting."

The compliment caught her off guard. For a second, she froze, her eyes softening before she quickly looked away. A small, almost shy smile tugged at her lips despite herself.

—

That night, Siya sat cross-legged on her bed, her phone glowing softly in her hand. On one app, she was speaking to Arav, who listened patiently, his questions full of care. On another screen, a waiting message blinked from Krunal:

Missing your voice. Can I call?

She couldn't help but smile.

"So, how was your day?" Arav's voice was warm, steady, the kind of comfort she had always leaned on.

"Hmm... it was okay," Siya said lightly. "Lovely and I went out for lunch... had a lot of laughs and fun."

"Are you happy there? Is everything okay?"

"Haan... everything is perfect," she replied softly, her voice a little too smooth, a little too careful.

They talked for a few more minutes, then hung up. Without hesitation, Siya tapped Krunal's name.

"Did you lie to Arav again today?" his voice came through, low and teasing, but not without meaning.

Her lips curled into a smirk. "What can I do? My day just doesn't feel complete without talking to you."

"So I'm the one who gets the harsh truth every night?" Krunal teased, his tone carrying a dangerous charm.

"Shhh... what if someone finds out?"

"I don't care. Do you?"

Siya hesitated, her thumb tracing idle patterns across the bedsheet. "...I don't know," she whispered, the words heavier than she intended.

The conversation drifted on, laughter blending with an unspoken undercurrent. Outside her window, the world was still, but inside the glow of her phone screen, Siya's eyes carried a spark—an energy, a thrill—one she hadn't given Arav in days.

Chapter 14 – Distance Grows

Evenings had begun to feel heavier for Arav.

That night, he sat on the edge of his bed, phone clutched tightly in his hand. The glow of the screen lit his tired face, his thumb hovering over the same chat window he had stared at for hours.

Last seen: 2 hours ago.

The words cut deeper than he cared to admit. His messages to Siya sat there—marked as Read. No reply.

With a heavy heart, he typed, each word weighing on his chest:

Is everything okay?

You're ignoring me...

Nothing feels the same anymore.

He waited. The little dots appeared—his breath hitched—then vanished. Silence.

The fan hummed overhead, the clock ticked on, but the room felt lifeless without her voice.

—-

Across the city, Shanti Memorial's staffroom was buzzing with brightness. Siya sat between Lovely and Krunal, her laughter bubbling out with ease, spilling into the air like a melody. The chatter of teachers, the clink of teacups, the rustle of papers—it all blended into a background where she looked... alive.

Her phone rested in her palm, lighting up with Arav's name. She didn't even glance at the message.

Lovely, catching the flash of the screen, raised her brows. "Your boyfriend is calling... ignoring him again?" Her tone was gentle, almost hesitant.

"Ugh yaar... the same questions every day," Siya sighed, waving her hand dismissively. "Arav has become so possessive. I'm tired now."

Just then, the phone buzzed again. Arav Calling. Without hesitation, Siya pressed End.

Krunal smirked, leaning closer. "Looks like someone's in high demand."

Siya rolled her eyes, trying to hide the flicker of guilt that crossed her face. "Bas... kuch bhi bolte ho."

But she didn't look back at her phone. Not once.

—-

Back in his darkened room, Arav tried again. No answer. The silence on the other end rang louder than any ringtone. He switched off the light, but sleep refused to come. The walls felt suffocating, the ceiling fan's hum unbearable.

Finally, he unlocked his phone again and typed:

You used to call me first.

Now even when I call, you're busy...

Tell me, Siya, what mistake did I make?

His thumb lingered over the screen before he hit Send. He stared at the chat, hoping for even a single word back. But none came.

—-

The next afternoon, the school canteen echoed with chatter. Siya sat at a corner table with Lovely and Krunal. The air smelled of fried snacks and cardamom tea. Krunal was in the middle of an animated story, his hands flying in the air as though he were on a stage. Siya's laughter rang out, warm and unrestrained, her eyes shining.

"Your smile is quite dangerous," Krunal teased with a smirk. "It steals hearts."

"You're too much, Krunal," she replied, swatting the air in mock protest. Her cheeks flushed, though she tried to mask it behind another laugh.

Lovely watched her quietly. Her own smile didn't quite reach her eyes. She leaned in, voice low so Krunal wouldn't hear. "Siya... did Arav call you last night?"

Siya's tone sharpened. "I feel pressured by his calls now, Lovely. He wants attention all the time. I just... need a little space."

Lovely didn't press further, but the unease lingered in her gaze.

—-

Days passed like this. Arav sat alone in his room, his phone always within reach. The silence on the screen had begun to seep into his bones. He hadn't heard Siya's voice in three days.

He finally recorded a voice note, his voice raw and low:

"Siya... can we talk? I need you. Everything feels empty without you."

He replayed it once before sending, then placed the phone face down on the bed. His eyes stung, his throat burned, but he refused to let the tears fall. He turned toward the framed family photo on his desk, searching for comfort in the frozen smiles. But even they looked blurred tonight.

—-

Meanwhile, in her own room, Siya lay sprawled against her pillows, idly scrolling through Instagram. A smile tugged at her lips as Krunal's latest post filled her screen—him holding a guitar, captioned with a witty line. She double-tapped without hesitation.

At the top of her screen, Arav's messages blinked again. She sighed.

"I just... need something else now," she muttered under her breath. "Arav ka pyaar suffocating lagta hai ab."

Without a second thought, she switched her phone to silent, the glow of the screen casting long shadows across her room. The world outside was still, but inside, the distance between her and Arav had grown into an unspoken chasm—one she no longer tried to bridge

—-

Chapter 15 – The Message That Broke the Sky

The evening light spilled into Arav's room like liquid gold, soft and warm, touching the edges of his bed, his books, his silent phone lying beside him. Outside, the sun bowed low, the world preparing for night. But inside, time itself seemed to move slower, heavier.

Arav sat cross-legged, scrolling through old chats with Siya. Each word, each emoji was a fragment of the life he thought they were still building together. There she was — smiling in that photo from their first trip, laughing in the little video she'd sent one rainy night when the power had gone out. "Arav, you're my light in the dark," her voice echoed faintly in his mind.

His lips curved into the faintest, aching smile. Then the phone buzzed.

A new message. From Siya.

He opened it without hesitation.

> My marriage has been fixed. With a boy from my own caste.

I'm not yours anymore. Please move on in your life.

Sorry, I can't continue this with you.

For a moment, the air froze. The world outside blurred — the barking of a stray dog, the faint honk of a rickshaw horn, the rustle of trees in the evening wind — all of it vanished. All that remained was the sharp, deafening thud of his own heartbeat.

His fingers stiffened around the phone. His throat went dry.

"This... this is a joke," he whispered, his voice trembling. His eyes darted across the words again and again, as if they would rearrange themselves into something kinder. "How could Siya... how could my Siya say this?"

His hands moved before his mind could catch up. He typed frantically:

> Siya, please... is this true?
You said you'd never marry anyone else.
We dreamed together, didn't we?
You said you loved me...
Please, talk to me. Don't break me like this.

The screen blinked. Seen.

No reply.

He called her. Once. Twice. Three times. Each ring stretched into eternity, each unanswered tone carving deeper into his chest.

"Please pick up," he muttered, voice breaking. "Just once. I'll make everything right. I'll fix everything, Siya. Please..."

Then — another ping. His breath caught. A new message.

> Don't interfere in my life.

And just like that, the words appeared like a knife across the screen: You have been blocked.

Arav stared, unblinking, his mind refusing to accept what his eyes were seeing. Then the golden light outside finally faded, leaving only the dark. His room swallowed him whole.

He sank to the floor, the phone clutched against his chest as though pressing it close could somehow bring her back. The tears came, first in silence, then unrelenting. His body shook with them, but the phone stayed against his heart — his last, useless lifeline.

In desperation, he searched her name again. Nothing. Profile gone. A void where her face used to be.

Hands trembling, he opened their gallery of memories — photos of her smile, screenshots of late-night calls, the video where she had leaned into the camera, eyes shining, and whispered: "I'll always be yours."

Arav's breath hitched violently. "So all of this... was a lie?" His voice cracked, small and broken, swallowed by the emptiness of the room.

His fist slammed into the wall, pain searing through his knuckles. But it was nothing compared to the tearing in his chest. He slid back against the wall, drained, his body heavy, his eyes burning.

And then, like an unwanted ghost, her voice echoed again — soft, tender, full of certainty.

"Arav, I never thought of anyone but you. You've become my whole life."

Now, there was only silence. Silence, and a phone that would never again light up with her name.

Chapter 16 – Another Conversation

That same night, miles away, Siya lay sprawled across her bed, the glow from her phone painting her face in soft blue light. The window was open, and the night breeze slipped in, carrying with it the faint scent of jasmine from the garden below. Her hair lifted gently with the wind, but her attention was fixed entirely on the screen in her hand.

At the top of her chat list, Krunal's name glowed. A small green dot pulsed beside it — online.

> Krunal: Finally, free from work. Can I call?

A slow smile curled onto her lips. Earlier, she had scrolled through Arav's messages — long, desperate paragraphs, his words spilling like a drowning man clinging to air. For a second, her chest had tightened with guilt. But almost as quickly, the feeling dissolved. Lately, his messages no longer warmed her; they weighed her down.

She pressed the call button.

"Hmm... finally," Krunal's voice came through, warm, teasing, carrying a casual intimacy. "I thought you forgot me tonight."

"Forget you?" Siya laughed softly, tucking herself deeper into her pillow. "That's impossible. You're... the only thing keeping me sane these days."

He chuckled, the sound low and easy. "And that boyfriend of yours? Did you tell him?"

Her smile faltered just for a moment. "I ended it."

There was silence, just the faint sound of his breath on the other end. Then, gently, "You actually told him about... us?"

"I told him my marriage was fixed," she cut in quickly, almost defensive. "It's easier this way. If I'd tried to explain... he would've begged, cried, pleaded for me to stay. I can't... I can't deal with that anymore."

Krunal's voice dropped lower, softer. "You're sure about this, Siya? No going back?"

Her eyes wandered across the dim room, landing on the corner of her desk. Behind a stack of books, half-hidden, stood a photo of her and Arav — his arm wrapped around her, both of them laughing, eyes bright with promises of forever. Something inside her pinched, sharp and fleeting.

"I'm sure," she whispered, though her throat tightened around the words. "I want... something else now."

The silence broke into laughter soon after. They drifted into stories, inside jokes, the rhythm of two people slipping into a world where nothing outside the call mattered. Siya's voice grew lighter, brighter, her laughter bubbling easily — laughter that had felt impossible in recent weeks with Arav. With Krunal, the air felt effortless, unburdened.

Outside, the moon climbed higher, silver light spilling over the sleeping streets. Inside, Siya's giggles filled the room, her face lit up as if nothing in the world had been broken.

But far away, in a darkened room with no laughter, Arav sat on the floor, staring at a silent phone pressed against his chest — waiting for a call that would never come again.

Chapter 17 – The Final Goodbye

The evening sky had dimmed into a cold, colorless gray, the drizzle outside tracing faint trails down the glass of Arav's window. Inside, the air felt heavier than the weather.

Arav sat slumped against the wall, knees pulled to his chest. His room was in quiet disarray—plates with untouched food on the desk, shirts hanging limply over a chair, books lying open as though abandoned mid-thought. His phone rested in his palm, its screen lit with the last photo Siya had ever sent him—her smiling in that pastel pink kurti, the one that always reminded him of spring.

He scrolled upwards through their old messages.

> "Mera babu ❤?"

"Never leave me, okay?"

"When you're with me, everything feels so simple..."

The words felt like they belonged to someone else's life, not his. The ache in his chest was deep and silent; no tears came, only the heaviness of being hollowed out.

A sudden ping broke the stillness.

A message from Lovely.

> Brother, please ask Siya to give me some time too. You both are always busy texting and calling.

Arav's brows drew together as he typed back.

> No sister... it's not me. Siya left me. Said her marriage is fixed and she blocked me from everywhere.

Minutes passed in silence. His heartbeat picked up, as if his body sensed something before his mind could.

> That's not possible. Every time I asked her whom she was talking to, she always said... "Arav."

He froze. The words felt like a loose thread in a tightly woven illusion. He didn't want to pull, but it was already unraveling.

—-

The next night, darkness pressed into his room. The only light came from his phone, washing his face in pale blue. He hadn't eaten. Sleep had been a stranger for days.

Another message from Lovely.

> Can we talk? Please call me — it's urgent.

His thumbs hovered.

> Is everything okay?

Just call. Please.

He hesitated, then pressed the call icon.

"Hello?" His voice was hoarse.

"Arav bro... can I ask you something?" Lovely's voice was low, cautious.

"Go ahead."

"I always thought Siya was busy on calls with you. She talked about you all the time—how you never let her be alone, how you were always connected."

A faint laugh escaped him, but there was no humor in it. "We haven't spoken in a week. Not a single text. She's ignoring me completely."

"What?" Lovely sounded stunned.

"Yeah. I thought maybe she was just busy... but now..." He trailed off.

Lovely was silent for a long moment before speaking again. "Then I was right. She's been lying to you. She wasn't talking to you... but she was smiling at her phone all day."

The truth landed sharp. "With someone else?"

"Yes. I didn't want to believe it earlier... but now I'm sure."

"No, Lovely," Arav said quickly, clinging to the story Siya had left him with. "Her marriage got fixed—with a guy from her caste. That's why she left."

"Bro... I'm sorry, but you're being fooled."

"Maybe she was talking to her fiancé—"

Lovely cut him off gently. "She never mentioned a fiancé at school. And... I never saw her call anyone except that guy—Krunal."

The name hit him like a slap.

"She was always with him," Lovely went on softly. "Walking together. Sitting together. Laughing like no one else existed. And every time I teased her, she just said, 'I'm talking to Arav.'"

"...She used my name to cover it?" His voice cracked.

"I didn't know until now. I'm sorry, bhai. I know how much you loved her."

Arav's breath slowed. "Lovely... can you do one last thing for me?"

"Yes. Anything."

"Ask her to talk to me. Just once. I won't beg. I just need one last goodbye."

—

An hour later, his phone lit up.

> Tell me. What do you want now?

His fingers trembled.

> Why did you do this to me, Siya? Why lie? Why cheat me like this? Why didn't you tell me it was Krunal?

The typing bubble appeared, vanished, then reappeared.

> So what? You made my life hell. You never let me wear western clothes. You were too emotional, too intense. I felt like I was drowning in your love. I needed space. Krunal gave me that.

His vision blurred.

> I can't live with you anymore. Please get out of my life. Don't come back. Goodbye.

He stared at the final word—how small it looked for something so final.

> I never thought you'd be the one to break me. But... thank you for showing me the truth. Goodbye, Siya. Be happy.

Setting the phone down, he walked to the window. Outside, the rain had started again—soft, unhurried, like his tears.

The world moved on in the distance.

But in Arav's room, time had stopped.

Chapter 18 – A New Dawn

Arav spent the next few weeks surrounded by his family. Their warmth became his medicine. His mother's gentle presence, his grandfather's wise stories, his younger brother's playful jokes—all stitched small patches of comfort on his broken heart.

But deep inside, the silence of his nights remained heavy. Songs that once reminded him of Siya now carried a different meaning. He no longer cried while listening to them—he simply sat still, letting the melodies flow through him like rivers carrying away the last traces of sorrow.

Slowly, he began to heal.

One evening, while sitting on the terrace under the fading light, Arav received an email. It was from an export company in Mumbai. "We are pleased to offer you the position..." The words lit something inside him. A spark of hope. A chance to start fresh in a new city.

He told his family, and though they were emotional about him leaving, they encouraged him. His mother hugged him tightly, whispering, "Beta, this is your new journey. Bhagwan tumhari raah banaye."

For the first time in months, Arav smiled genuinely.

—-

Parallel Thread – Siya and Krunal

While Arav prepared for his new life, Siya's days took a different turn. At her new school, Krunal became her constant companion. They laughed together in the staff room, shared lunch, and often stayed back after classes discussing work, sometimes even personal dreams.

It wasn't dramatic, not like a storm. It was slow and subtle—two people simply leaning toward each other in ways neither admitted aloud. Siya, who once clung to Arav's voice late at night, now found herself waiting for Krunal's texts. She told herself it was harmless. She told herself it was friendship. But deep down, she knew it was more.

And every time her phone buzzed with Krunal's message, she replied instantly—unlike the way she had once delayed Arav's calls.

—-

On the morning of his departure, Arav touched his mother's feet, his eyes filled with both gratitude and pain. With his bag slung over his shoulder, he looked back at his family one last time before boarding the train.

As the train pulled out of the station, the world outside blurred into streaks of color. Arav leaned his head against the window and whispered to himself, "This is not the end. This is a new beginning."

And while Arav moved toward an uncertain yet hopeful future in Mumbai, Siya drifted further into Krunal's orbit, unknowingly writing a different chapter of her life.

Chapter 19 — Where She Ended, I Begin

The morning air of Mumbai clung heavy with the metallic scent of railway tracks and the chatter of a thousand rushing footsteps. The local train screeched into the platform, steel grinding against steel, and the crowd surged forward with practiced urgency.

Arav moved against that tide—not resisting it, not flowing with it—just moving slowly, as if time around him had lost its pace. A small, worn bag hung from his shoulder, light yet heavy with the weight of unspoken thoughts. His eyes carried a tiredness that had nothing to do with sleepless nights; it was the quiet exhaustion of a heart that had loved and been left behind.

Finding a seat near the window, he sat without a word. The train jolted forward, and the city outside began to smear into a moving canvas—high-rises casting long, solemn shadows, narrow lanes where chai stalls already steamed in the awakening sun, and the golden morning struggling to pierce the thick veil of smog.

Memories struck without warning.

Laughter under the rain, dripping from umbrellas and clothes clinging to skin.

Two cups of tea in the staff room, fingers brushing as they reached for the same spoon.

Hands held in secret, hearts beating like conspirators in the quiet of stolen moments.

Her smile—the one she no longer reserved for him.

The present blurred. In his mind, he was elsewhere, seated on a wooden bench in a quiet park at sunset. The golden light softened everything, but it could not touch the ache inside him. The breeze was gentle, birds sang somewhere far away, and yet his hands were clasped tight, as if holding himself together.

There was a time...

His own voice echoed in the hollow chambers of his thoughts.

A time when she had been terrified of losing me. When I had that accident, she cried as though the world itself had ended. She held me like I was her entire universe.

He tilted his head back, staring at the pale sky visible through the train's grimy window.

And now... she doesn't even care if I live or die.

A pause. A swallow. His jaw tightened, holding back the weight of words that refused to leave.

It's true what they say... when a third person enters, a relationship doesn't grow stronger—it begins to crack. Everyone chases a better option. A richer boy. A more successful man.

A single tear betrayed him, tracing a line down his cheek.

And I... I was the fool who dared to fall in true love... in a world full of false people.

The memory receded, leaving him back in the rattling train. He exhaled long and slow, eyes moist but refusing to spill over. His phone glowed in his palm. He scrolled through old photographs—school trip selfies, a birthday candlelit by laughter, the first "I love you" in text form.

"Was it all a lie, Siya?" he murmured under his breath.

The phone rang. Maa.

He hesitated just a fraction of a second before answering.

"Yes, Mom... I've reached. Sitting in the train. It's about to leave. Everything's fine—don't worry."

Her voice, warm yet tinged with concern, crackled through the line.

"Take care of yourself, son. If you need anything, tell me."

He smiled faintly, though she couldn't see it.

"Yes... I'm fine, Mom."

When the call ended, he closed his eyes briefly. A child beside him dropped a small plastic toy onto the floor. Arav bent, picked it up, and handed it back.

"Bhaiya, aap udaas ho?" the boy asked, his innocent curiosity cutting through the train's din.

Arav gave a slight shake of his head. "No."

Then he turned back to the window. The glass reflected a version of himself that was quieter now, but not defeated.

Jahan usne khatam kiya... wahin se main shuru karunga.

The city blurred past, the train cutting through Mumbai's veins like a lifeline. It carried people, stories, heartbreaks, and beginnings. And it carried him too—away from where he had been, toward where he had yet to go.

Chapter 20 — To Find Myself Again

The night air at Marine Drive was cool, tinged with the salt of the Arabian Sea. Streetlights cast soft golden halos in the puddles left behind by an earlier drizzle, their reflections trembling as the waves pushed and pulled against the shore. The city hummed in the distance—cars passing, voices rising and falling—but here, near the water, the sound softened into a quiet murmur.

Arav walked slowly along the promenade. A simple shirt, worn jeans, and the weight of a day heavier than most clung to him like a second skin. His eyes were puffy from the tears he hadn't wanted to shed, yet his steps remained steady, deliberate. Couples dotted the path—hands intertwined, heads resting on shoulders, sharing private laughter that rose and dissolved into the breeze.

He passed them, alone... but not lost.

His feet carried him to his usual spot—a broken stone ledge facing the sea. He lowered himself onto it, the cold stone pressing through his jeans. The wind lifted strands of his hair, mingling the scent of wet earth and salt in the air. Before him, the ocean stretched into darkness, vast and endless, its surface glimmering faintly under the city lights.

Pyar zaroori tha... par khud ko sambhalna usse bhi zaroori tha.

(Love was important... but holding myself together was even more important.)

He breathed deeply, as if the night air could sweep away the remnants of pain. From his pocket, he drew out his phone. An old photograph lit the screen—Siya and him, faces pressed together, eyes bright with a happiness that now felt like it belonged to strangers.

His thumb hovered over the screen. The phone asked, Are you sure?

A single tear escaped down his cheek. He wiped it away quickly, as though it had no right to be there, and pressed Yes.

Kabhi socha tha... jiske liye sab kuch chhod diya, aaj usi ke liye khud ko chhod baitha tha.

(I once left everything for her... and in the process, I almost left myself.)

Lifting his gaze, he searched the sky. Through the haze of city lights and smog, a few stubborn stars still twinkled—small, but defiant.

Ab khud se wapas milne ka waqt hai.

(Now... it's time to meet myself again.)

A smile touched his lips, gentle and unforced. It felt unfamiliar at first, but it stayed.

A child's laughter rang out nearby. Arav looked down to see a little boy chasing a paper boat that had wandered toward him on a thin stream of rainwater. The boat stopped at his feet. He picked it up, noticing the uneven scrawl of a crayon across its side:

Zindagi khoobsurat hai.

(Life is beautiful.)

His smile deepened—soft, calm, healing.

Toote dil ke tukdon se... naye khwab bunte hain. Aur main... ab sapne dekhna chahta hoon.

(From broken pieces of a heart... new dreams are stitched. And I... want to dream again.)

The waves kept their rhythm. The city kept moving. But for the first time in a long while, Arav felt still—anchored not in someone else's love, but in his own strength.

Far ahead, the sea merged with the night, and somewhere in that meeting of darkness and water, he found the quiet promise of beginnings—fragile, bright, and entirely his own.

Acknowledgements

This novel, Woh Ek Saal, is more than just a story—it is a piece of my heart. Writing it was not a journey I made alone.

First and foremost, I am deeply grateful to my family, whose love and support kept me strong during the entire process. Their patience and encouragement gave me the courage to keep writing, even when the road felt uncertain.

A heartfelt thanks to my friends, who believed in me and reminded me that dreams are worth chasing. Your honest feedback, warm words, and constant motivation shaped this book in more ways than you will ever know.

To my readers—thank you for choosing to spend your time with my words. It is your love for stories that inspires me to continue writing. This book is dedicated to everyone who has ever loved deeply, lost painfully, and found the strength to begin again.

About the Author

Prashant Bhardwaj is an emerging storyteller from India, passionate about weaving emotional, romantic, and dramatic narratives that connect with the heart. His inspiration for writing comes from real emotions, everyday struggles, and the timeless beauty of love and loss.

Woh Ek Saal is his debut novel, a heartfelt tale that reflects his belief in the power of relationships and the resilience of the human spirit.

When he is not writing, Prashant enjoys traveling, listening to music, and watching movies—simple joys that fuel his imagination.

With every story he writes, his dream is to touch lives, heal hearts, and remind readers that even after the darkest nights, a new morning always arrives.

Woh Ek Saal

One year of love. One year of trust. One year that changed everything.
Arav believed Siya was his forever. Their love was young, pure, and unshakable—or so he thought. But when unexpected truths surface, his world collapses, leaving behind questions, heartbreak, and the painful journey of letting go.
Woh Ek Saal is an emotional tale of love, betrayal, and self-discovery. A story that reminds us: sometimes the hardest goodbyes are the ones that teach us who we really are.

Don't miss out!

Visit the website below and you can sign up to receive emails whenever Prashant Bhardwaj publishes a new book. There's no charge and no obligation.

https://books2read.com/r/B-A-QKLNE-OGEKI

BOOKS 2 READ

Connecting independent readers to independent writers.

About the Author

Prashant Bhardwaj is a storyteller at heart, passionate about exploring the complexities of human emotions, love, and relationships. With a deep understanding of heartbreak, hope, and self-discovery, he brings characters to life in a way that resonates with readers across generations.

When he's not writing, Prashant enjoys traveling, listening to music, and observing the small, meaningful moments of everyday life that inspire his stories. Tere Baad is his latest work, reflecting his signature style of heartfelt drama and poignant romance.

Read more at https://www.instagram.com/achintyawritingpage?igsh=MTI0czZ1YjBqcDh6MQ==.

www.ingramcontent.com/pod-product-compliance
Lightning Source LLC
LaVergne TN
LVHW090431210926
848480LV00002B/781
9798230357759